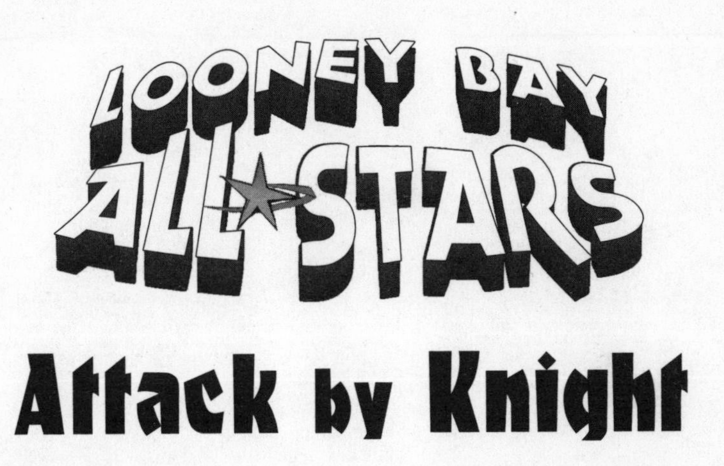

Attack by Knight

Attack by Knight

Helaine Becker

Illustrated by
Sampar

Scholastic Canada Ltd.
Toronto New York London Auckland Sydney
Mexico City New Delhi Hong Kong Buenos Aires

Scholastic Canada Ltd.
604 King Street West, Toronto, Ontario M5V 1E1, Canada

Scholastic Inc.
557 Broadway, New York, NY 10012, USA

Scholastic Australia Pty Limited
PO Box 579, Gosford, NSW 2250, Australia

Scholastic New Zealand Limited
Private Bag 94407, Greenmount, Auckland, New Zealand

Scholastic Children's Books
Euston House, 24 Eversholt Street, London NW1 1DB, UK

Thank you to Andrew McKay for helping the All-Stars out with their lacrosse game!

Library and Archives Canada Cataloguing in Publication
Becker, Helaine, 1961-
Attack by knight / Helaine Becker ; illustrated by Sampar.
(Looney Bay All-Stars)
ISBN 0-439-94621-2
I. Sampar II. Title. III. Series.
PS8553.E295532A88 2006 jC813'.6 C2006-902253-4

6 5 4 3 2 1 Printed in Canada 06 07 08 09 10

Contents

Chapter 1

"And this is how people in medieval times darned socks..."

As the tour guide droned on, Reese McSkittles trailed behind the rest of his class. He usually thought field trips were fun, but that wasn't the case today.

For one thing, he was in an awful mood. The day before, the All-Stars had been thoroughly crushed at lacrosse by

their arch-rivals, the Trinity Bay Marauders. Reese was still smarting from the loss — especially since the Marauders had cheated.

For another thing, the Museum of the Middle Ages was giving him the creeps. It was dark and gloomy and full of old things. It reminded him of the time he'd been locked up in the hold of a pirate ship.

All in all, he felt bored, miserable and trapped.

Reese rummaged around in his pocket for an old coin he'd found at the hockey rink. He had hoped that someone at the museum could tell him more about it. He'd tried to ask the guide, but she just yelled at him for interrupting her lecture on cheese-making.

Reese turned the coin between his fingers, feeling the bashed rim and the outline of the roaring lion on its face. Touching its smooth, cool surface somehow made him feel better. The whole

class sighed with misery as the guide launched into a lecture on medieval pig-keeping. *At this rate*, Reese thought, *I'll never get a chance to ask about my coin!*

That's when he noticed a door with a sign on it that said *Staff Only*.

Reese cut a quick glance at his teacher, Mr. Norman. He and the guide were discussing pig breeds of the Middle Ages. Their backs were to the group. This was his chance! Reese darted through the door. Maybe someone else on the museum's staff would know more about the coin.

Reese found himself in a dank, musty hall. Dull suits of armour stood on guard along both sides. As he walked between the rows, the eyeholes in the helmets seemed to wink at him. He kept a tight grip on the coin for comfort.

Reese tried to imagine how it would feel to wear all that heavy armour. *I'll never complain about my lacrosse*

pads again, he thought.

He stood in front of a suit that had a battle-axe clasped in its glove. He could almost hear the clash of metal on metal.

Just for a goof, Reese pretended to swing a broadsword at the knight. "Take that, you can of tuna!"

Suddenly, a ringing voice said, "Pray, desist your foolery!"

The voice had come from the suit of armour!

"Oh, wow," Reese squeaked. "You're alive!"

"Of course I am alive," the knight said. "Dost thou think a suit of armour can walk and talk of its own will?"

"N-n-no," stammered Reese. "But there's not supposed to be anyone inside the armour. It's for display. I didn't think we were allowed to play in it."

"Play? I am Sir Waverly of Waverton, the Queen's own knight. I have vanquished entire armies, laid siege to mighty kingdoms and claimed great lands in the name of my Lady. I do *not* play!" He lifted the visor on his helmet to reveal a stern set of eyes. "Why, I was just in the midst of a fierce duel to the

death, when…" Sir Waverly's voice dropped off. "How strange, I cannot recall what happened next. The last thing I remember is Sir Hugh roaring toward me on his steed…"

"And I was about to give you what for, too! *Twit!*" a new voice boomed. Reese spun around and saw another knight striding toward him, his sword raised.

Reese moaned. It had happened again!

Chapter 2

The second knight stopped in front of Reese and lowered his sword. Reese couldn't believe his eyes. First pirates, now knights! Why couldn't history stay where it belonged? In the past. At least the knights hadn't threatened to kidnap him. Yet. And they certainly smelled better than the pirates.

"Hugh!" shouted Sir Waverly.

"Did you think you could escape me

by some foul magic? I had thee in my sights, and then you disappeared. Now I find myself here, in this strange place..." Sir Hugh glared at Reese and the other suits of armour. "'Tis no matter! I have you now!" Sir Hugh raised his blade again.

"Whoa!" said Reese. "Put that sword away. Someone could get hurt!"

"I think that's the idea, boy," hissed Sir Waverly.

Reese thought quickly. "The museum's rules of engagement state that weapons may not be drawn on museum property without written permission."

"Is that so?" Sir Hugh slid his sword into its scabbard. "Then where can I take this clobberhead to slay him?"

"You can't *slay* anybody. Things have

changed quite a bit since you've been…er… away."

Sir Hugh looked down at Reese. "Away? Do you know how we came to be here, stripling? If so, speak now."

Reese spoke quickly, "I don't know how. Weird things just happen to me. A minute ago I walked into this room, and *poof!*" He snapped his fingers. "Suits of armour that have been empty for hundreds of years weren't empty anymore. You guys must be over 500 years old! I really don't know how you got here. Honest."

"Where exactly is *here?*" Sir Hugh demanded.

"In Newfoundland, at the Museum of the Middle Ages. It's the twenty-first century," Reese replied.

"I have never heard of this Newfoundland," said Sir Waverly. "Are the winters nice? England can be so damp—"

"Enough!" Sir Hugh roared. "I do not care a jot about where or when we are. I just want to run you through. Now, you, boy — what do they call you?" he asked.

"Reese McSkittles, sir."

"Ah," said Sir Waverly, "a member of the Skittles clan. Why, I know your countrymen: Crispin of Coffey, Dudley of Melk, Sir Kit of Kat..."

Sir Hugh ignored him. "McSkittles, I command you to take us to the battlefield at once!"

Just then Reese heard a door slam. "Oh, no! We can't let anyone see you." He pushed Sir Waverly back against the wall. "Stand still and don't talk," he told them both.

"I've never hidden from anyone in my life!" Sir Hugh began. "I will not start now!"

"Shhh!" hissed Reese. "You'd *better*

start now. If you tell people you're a knight from the Middle Ages, they'll lock you up! Now, just wait here until I come back. If you behave, I promise to take you some place nice to bash each other."

He heard another door slam and then voices. Reese glared at Sir Hugh until he move back against the wall. Then Reese slipped out to find his class.

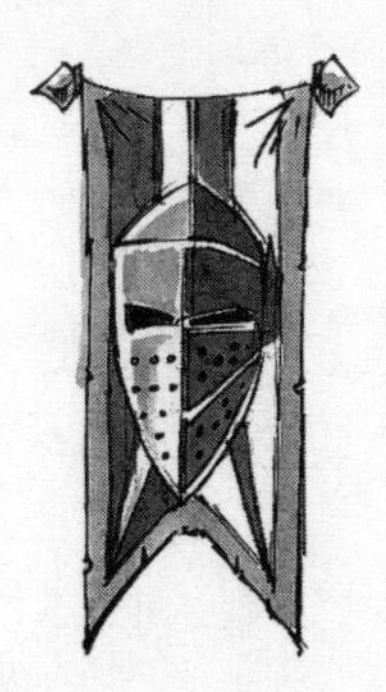

Chapter 3

"Where did you disappear to?" Darren Willett whispered as Reese stepped into place beside him. The tour had just ended.

"You're never going to believe this..." Reese began.

"Hold that thought," said Darren, pointing to the doorway.

Another field-trip group was filtering into the museum. In the group were

three boys whom Reese and Darren knew well — too well. They were Seamus Snodgrass and his bully boy buddies, Jack Patrick and Roman Quaig. They were the top players for the Trinity Bay Marauders.

"I smell trouble," said Reese.

It wasn't long before Seamus and his friends spotted the Looney Bay kids and came over. Seamus bumped into Laura Hook, hard. She was knocked to her knees.

"Pardon me, Cap'n Hook," Seamus taunted. "Seems you're just as much a

pushover off the lacrosse floor as you are on it."

Laura scowled at Seamus as she got back on her feet. "And I guess you use the same dirty moves off the floor as you do on it. You think you're so great because you cheated your way to a cheap win yesterday? We would have beat you hands down if you hadn't kept fouling us when the ref wasn't looking."

"Aw, wittle Waura didn't want to get her dress dirty?" mocked Seamus. Jack and Roman guffawed.

Reese spoke up. "Laura's right. You didn't play fair, and you didn't deserve the win."

"Oh really? And you did?"

"We did," said Shannon Weiss, also joining the fray.

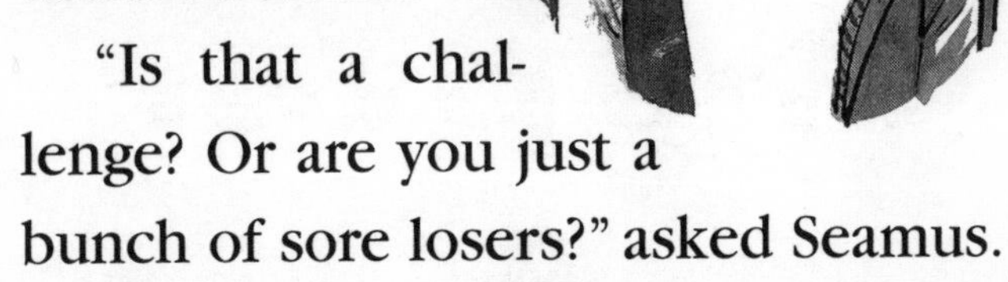

"We could beat you fair and square, no question about it," declared Laura.

"Is that a challenge? Or are you just a bunch of sore losers?" asked Seamus.

"What do you think, guys? Is that a challenge?" Laura glanced at Shannon, at Reese and at Darren. They each nodded.

"Where and when?" she demanded.

"After school. Your arena," said Seamus. "Prepare to feel the pain. Again."

Chapter 4

Reese was starting to panic. Mr. Norman was herding the class back to the bus. With all of the excitement over the rematch, Reese still hadn't figured out what to do with Sir Waverly and Sir Hugh.

"Um, guys," he began. "I have to do something. Can you cover for me?"

"Reese, you have to come with us!" Shannon looked a little panicked herself. "Your mum said she'd shred all of us into lobster salad if you disappeared again."

"Don't worry, I'll meet you at the pirates' arena by four. Promise." Reese sped back into the museum before his friends could stop him.

When he reached the *Staff Only* door again, he took a look around, and then slipped through it. He walked between the rows of armour until he saw two gaps.

The knights were gone.

Had they somehow gone back to where they had come from? Reese crossed his fingers and called out, "Sir Waverly? Sir Hugh? Hey, ya old tin cans, are you here?"

Nothing. A huge grin spread across Reese's face.

He raced back to the museum's exit just in time to see his bus disappear. He had a long walk ahead of him, but he was too relieved to care.

As Reese hit the museum's long driveway, he began to whistle happily. He thought he heard a shout. He decided to ignore it and whistled louder. Then he heard a series of metallic clanks, and he whistled even louder.

Soon Reese heard what could have only been a battle cry, then the sound of swords clashing. And since he couldn't whistle any louder, he gave a deep sigh and went to see what was going on.

There, in a clearing beside the driveway, a fierce battle raged.

"Take that, you mewling son of a sheep!" *Clash!* Sir Waverly's sword met Sir Hugh's.

"Ha! Is that the best you can do, you artless donkey cart?" Sir Hugh parried. Sir Waverly lunged at him, but Sir Hugh neatly ducked the attack. Sir Waverly went sprawling in the dirt.

Maybe it wasn't such a fierce battle after all.

"Lout! Pimple on a hog's bottom!" Sir

Waverly bellowed. He rolled on the ground, trying to get up.

Reese figured it was time to step in. "Hey, I thought I told you to stay put. Plus, you're still on museum property. You don't have permission to duel here."

"My honour would not allow me to stand by while this foul wretch still

breathed. Now step aside, whelp!" Sir Hugh raised his weapon, but waited as Sir Waverly tried to struggle to his feet.

"I'm sorry to break the rules, McSkittles," Sir Waverly apologized. "But I've been challenged, and I cannot turn my back on a challenge."

A challenge?

"Wait!" said Reese. "I think I have an idea." He knew what it was like to have your honour at stake. And he'd never been able to back down from a challenge either. "I know a way that you can finish your challenge and play by the rules. But you'll have to come with me."

"You will help us settle our dispute?" said Sir Waverly. "How?"

Reese smiled. "Have you ever played lacrosse?"

Chapter 5

It was 3:45 p.m. The school day was over.

The Looney Bay All-Stars and the Trinity Bay Marauders were already warming up at the arena. The All-Stars were getting worried about Reese — and about what his mother might do if he went missing again.

Darren was the first to spot him. Then he saw the knights. "Hey guys, here comes Reese. And he's not alone."

The All-Stars and the Marauders watched in amazement as Reese and the knights walked into the arena.

It had been a long walk back. Cars had kept honking as they passed. The first vehicle had been an eighteen-wheeler. It had sent Sir Waverly into the ditch, screaming about dragons. Sir

Hugh, on the other hand, had run after it for some time, hoping to attack its underbelly.

"This is our arena," Reese said now.

"Is that like a jousting field? Or a duelling ground?" Sir Waverly asked.

"Pretty much," Reese replied.

"Ah-ha!" said Sir Hugh. "At last! Again, I challenge you to a duel to the death!"

"And I accept your challenge, again, you gorbellied half-wit!" Sir Waverly shot back.

By this time they had reached the All-Stars' bench. As the knights traded insults, Reese huddled with his friends and quickly explained what had happened at the museum. The All-Stars, who had once played a hockey game to save Reese from pirates, weren't that surprised. Then Reese told them about the knights' feud and his plan to help end it.

The huddle broke, and Laura walked over to Sir Waverly and Sir Hugh. "Look, you guys. We don't duel to the death any more."

"Then how do you resolve matters of honour?" asked Sir Hugh.

"Well, we play a game," Laura replied. "See who the winner is. Like right now, it's lacrosse season. We have rivalries with other schools and we play matches against them. The winners get bragging rights. And a trophy."

Darren said, "This afternoon we challenged Snotty Snodgrass and his gang up at Trinity Bay Prep School to a rematch. We start in a few minutes. We play four ten-minute quarters. If there's a tie, then it's sudden-death overtime."

Sir Hugh perked up. "Ah! So there *is* proper duelling and killing. Thank goodness!"

"Sudden death just means that whoever scores the first goal in overtime wins it all," Reese explained.

"Pfft," Sir Hugh muttered.

"So, are you saying that instead of a sword fight, we play this lacrosse amusement to the 'sudden death?'" asked Sir Waverly.

Reese nodded.

"How do you play?"

"It's pretty simple," Laura said. She grabbed a paper and pencil from her bag, and drew a box floor and a lacrosse stick.

"You try to score points by getting your ball into the other team's goal. You use the head end of your stick to carry and throw the ball — you can't touch the ball with your hands."

"The other end, is it to clout the enemy over the head?" asked Sir Hugh hopefully.

"No!" Laura said crossly. "Just pay attention, won't you?"

"Sorry," said Sir Hugh.

She continued her explanation. "The goalie protects the net. There are five runners that defend against the other team's attackers. The attackers try to advance the ball by passing it back and forth until they can shoot. If the defenders stop the attackers and get the ball, they attack the other team's goal. Are you with me so far?" Laura asked. The knights nodded.

"Good. The winning team is the one that scores the most goals before the clock runs out."

Sir Waverly asked, "And you will allow us to join your teams?"

Reese looked at his friends. "We'll have to get the Marauders to agree to take one of them."

"Consider it done," Darren said. He went off to explain the situation to the Marauders. Actually, he made up a situation — they never would have believed the truth.

"This is perfect," said Reese. "Now

you can help us settle things with the Marauders, and we'll help you settle things with each other."

Sir Waverly turned to Sir Hugh. "The knight with the winning team shall be declared the victor. The loser shall, of course, face exile. The matter of honour will have been settled. Dost thou agree to the terms, Sir Hugh?"

Sir Hugh nodded. "If this is the way they settle matters of honour in this strange land, then yes, I agree. Sir Waverly, prepare to meet thy doom in the battle of lacrosse!"

Chapter 6

The teams met in the centre zone. Darren was holding a few thin strands of dry grass upright in his fist. The knights would draw straws to pick their teams. Seamus Snodgrass was standing beside Darren, his usual sneer plastered on his face. He beckoned Sir Hugh and Sir Waverly over. Darren had told him they were players from a senior team, the Fighting Knights. They were here to make sure the teams played fair.

"May the best man win — by choosing the Marauders," Seamus boasted.

Sir Waverly and Sir Hugh each drew a straw. Sir Waverly's was longer.

"I choose to play on the All-Stars," he said, flicking the straw at Seamus. "I am not overfond of braggarts."

The two teams took their places on

the floor. Sir Hugh and Sir Waverly positioned themselves for the faceoff.

The ref blew the whistle.

"*Attack!*" shouted Sir Hugh. He lunged, wielding his lacrosse stick like a duelling sword.

Sir Waverly nimbly turned Sir Hugh's stick aside. He thrust and Sir Hugh parried, then Sir Waverly thrust again. The ref blew his whistle over and over again, but the knights didn't notice.

All of a sudden, Sir Hugh stuck out his foot. Sir Waverly fell over it and landed with a thud, flat on his back.

With a raucous, "Ah-*HA!*" Sir Hugh

stepped on Sir Waverly's belly, pinning him in place. He pointed the stick's head at Sir Waverly's throat. Only then did it sink in that they had been

duelling with lacrosse sticks, not swords.

"Dash it all," Sir Hugh said. "I would have run you through on the spot if I'd had my trusty sword, Ex Camembert."

"You couldn't run me through if I were a tunnel," jibed Sir Waverly. He picked himself up and dusted off his backside.

The ref scurried over, blowing and blowing his whistle. "You both get two-minute penalties for slashing. And for not listening," he said huffily.

Play went on without the knights, and by the end of the first quarter, the score was tied at 1.

At the second quarter, Sir Waverly took command of the All-Stars.

"The cavalry will come up on the left flank," he ordered, "and the bowmen will send volleys up the right. Then I'll charge up the middle and take the victory."

"Lacrosse isn't really played that way," said Darren.

"Besides, we don't have cavalry. Or archers," Reese pointed out.

The knight waved them off. "I am a master strategist. Why, just last year this very battle plan won me my favourite castle. It has two moats."

The rest of his team rolled their eyes, but took up their positions. The All-Stars' right-handers lined up on the left,

prepared to charge. The lefties took their positions on the right.

But Sir Hugh had a battle plan of his own. He won the faceoff and took control of the ball. Then, with the lacrosse

stick tucked under his arm like a lance, he began his charge into the defensive zone.

He blew past the All-Stars' runners and advanced on Darren in net.

Still charging, Sir Hugh raised his stick overhead like a mace. Once, twice, three times it twirled.

And Darren, seeing the fierce look in the knight's eyes, decided that he'd like to keep his head. He leapt aside.

With a laugh, Sir Hugh stopped twirling his stick, walked up to the goal and calmly slung the ball into the net.

The score was now 2–1 for the Marauders.

Chapter 7

In the third and fourth quarters, Sir Waverly and Sir Hugh actually started to play real lacrosse. They might not have had a great handle on the rules, but they had power and determination.

Both teams played hard — harder than they'd ever played before. Reese was grateful when the whistle finally blew. The score was tied at 3–3.

Reese dropped down heavily on the

bench and sluiced some water over his head. Then he passed the bottle to Sir Waverly.

"The battle goes well," Sir Waverly said grimly. "It will not be long before that loathsome lout is vanquished for all time."

Reese shook his head.

"I just don't get it. Why the heck are you so mad at each other? I mean, how bad could it be?"

Sir Waverly squared his massive shoulders. "Why? 'Tis simple. Because he abandoned his armies on the battlefield. Because he betrayed his queen — and his own *brother* — when he left us to beat back the foe alone."

"You mean Sir Hugh is your brother?" asked Shannon, astounded.

"If you could call that coxcomb a brother, yes."

"It's not like I left of my own will, you cretin! You drove me to it, you did!" shouted Sir Hugh over the bench divider.

"I drove you to it?"

"It's what you said. I heard you, Wavy.

Don't deny it," said Sir Hugh.

"You're raving, man! I know nothing of what you speak."

"Oh, really?" snorted Sir Hugh. "You don't recall telling your friend Sir Dunstan that I smell?"

"Don't be ridiculous, Hugh! I did nothing of the sort!"

"You did! I heard you loud and clear. We were under attack at Dunedin, and you said, 'Hugh smells like an overweight donkey.'"

"I never said you smell. In fact, you are the least odiferous knight I know." Sir Waverly thought for a moment. "Oh, wait, I think I know what you might have heard. Just before you deserted us at Dunedin, Dunstan tripped and landed in a most awkward way. I laughed and said, 'You fell like an over laden-donkey.' Yes. That's what I said. I swear it."

Sir Hugh fidgeted. "Well…um… Nothing but a silly mistake then, I guess. You know, I only left the battlefield because you hurt my feelings."

"You should know I'd never do that! Not on purpose, anyway!"

Sir Hugh wiped away a tear. "I'm so sorry, Wavy."

Sir Waverly reached over the Plexiglas and took Sir Hugh's hand in his.

"Brother..."

"Friend..."

The two knights went off to patch things up.

"Such a pretty scene," Seamus sneered. "But some of us have a tie to break. Which of you *losers* is coming?"

Reese stood up. "For sudden death? We're in. And then we'll see who the real losers are."

The Marauders put Seamus in for the faceoff. The All-Stars put in Laura. They

17
2

glared at each other across the centre line.

Reese took a deep breath and set himself in position. Rocking lightly on his toes, he readied himself for a fast break in any direction.

The ref blew the whistle.

One Eyed-Elmer, who'd been watching from the stands, turned on the sound system for the play-by-play. His voice came loud and clear over the speakers.

"Hook touches the ball first for the All-Stars, but, argh, *she's unable to take control. Snodgrass scoops it up. He passes long to Patrick, who shoots! It's a*

sizzler to the upper left corner! Knocked away by Willett!

"McSkittles picks the ball up at the attack line. He's looking for an open player. He's found Weiss. Weiss to Wetherbury to Hook. She shoots! It's — no good. Wide.

"Now Trinity has control. The All-Stars go to one-on-one defence. The Marauders can't get a clear shot. Snodgrass fakes left — and a fast pass to the right! Quaig's

made the catch, he's going for the goal! Oh! That was close, but Willett makes a brilliant shoulder save to keep the ball in play.

"Willett passes to Hook, Hook to McSkittles to Weiss. Weiss dekes to go deep into the attack zone. But she's blocked. Weiss flicks a short pass to McSkittles. The pass is low! McSkittles can't get it! Snodgrass nabs it for the Marauders… What's this? He's dropped it! Snodgrass has dropped the ball!

"McSkittles is in a clinch with Snodgrass, struggling for control. McSkittles knocks it free! What a great move! It's skimming across the floor to Hook. She

scoops and — whoa! *What a shot! The ball slams into the goal! It's an All-Star victory!"*

A deafening cheer rose up from the All-Stars. Seamus Snodgrass threw down his stick and pulled off his gloves.

"Why, you weasels!" he bellowed, and went for Reese.

Sir Hugh leapt onto the floor from the stands. He lifted Seamus by his collar. "Hold up, young man! You have lost the battle fairly. Honour dictates that you concede victory. Now apologize."

"Yes sir," said Seamus weakly. He turned to Reese. "Ever so sorry."

Sir Hugh put Seamus down.

The All-Stars cheered as the Trinity Bay Marauders slunk out of the arena.

Chapter 8

Reese and Darren started home.

"What's going to happen to the knights?" Darren asked.

"Oh, I got them all set up with the pirates. Seems Sir Hugh and Sir Waverly always wanted to operate a 'publick faire.' You know, like a theme park: 'Medieval Knights — Join the Joust!' Sir Hugh and Black-and-Bluebeard are putting together a business plan now."

"That doesn't sound so good, Reese."

"Why?"

"You tell me," replied Darren. He pointed.

Under the parking lot lights, they could see Captain Black-and-Bluebeard and Sir Hugh, each with a glinting sword in his hand, thrusting and parrying.

Black-and-Bluebeard's gravelly voice floated to them. He was cursing Sir Hugh: "Why you yellow-bellied, cheating, landlubbering sand-flea!"

Sir Hugh roared back, "How dare you try to deceive me, barnacle-breath!"

Reese laughed. "I guess they're like the All-Stars and the Marauders."

Darren agreed. "It's going to be a long, hard battle, then..."